For Sally, an angel of a friend MM
For Nikita, with love and cuddles SR

Martine Murray and Sally Rippin both write
and illustrate books. Since they are friends,
they wanted to make a book together. This is it.

Martine's other books include the Henrietta series
and the Cedar B. Hartley books. Sally's books
include *Where is Baby?* and *Gezani and the Tricky
Baboon*, written by Valanga Khoza. Visit her
website at www.sallyrippin.com

MANNIE AND THE
LONG BRAVE DAY

Martine Murray
and Sally Rippin

ALLEN&UNWIN

Here's Mannie.
She's wearing her ladybug dress.

And here's Strawberry Luca.
She has no clothes on, so Mannie
wraps her in a tea towel.

Here's Lilliput. Lilliput is too shy
for dressing up.

Mannie has a special box.
It's full of secret things.

Where are you going, Mannie?
'We're going on an adventure.'

Lilliput says, 'I'm scared.'
'Come on, Lilliput,' says Mannie.
'Be brave. You're a big girl now.'

Mannie pulls noses of people she loves,
even elephant noses.

'We're skip trip skipping down
the old rocky road . . .'

Wait a minute! What's in the box?

'Look, it's sparkly shoes for Strawberry Luca.'

'We're creep peep creeping through the tall reaching trees . . .'

Wait a minute! What's in the box?

'Look, it's a serious explorer hat for Lilliput.'

'We're splish splash splishing through the wild winding river ...'

Wait a minute! What's in the box?

'Look, it's a famous stripy umbrella
for everyone to squeeze into.'

'We're stomp clomp stomping
up the high lonely hill ...'

Wait a minute! What's in the box?

'It's a woolly old blanket for our picnic.'

Oh dear, the sun has
hidden behind a cloud.

It's dark.

And cold.

And quiet.

Strawberry Luca has lost one of her sparkly shoes. They huddle under the old woolly blanket. The sky rumbles.

'I'm scared,' says Mannie.
Her ladybird wings tremble.

'Wait a minute,' says Lilliput.
'What's in the box?'

'Look, it's a ladder.'

Lilliput takes a big brave breath and climbs carefully up the ladder. She wobbles and sways and takes another big brave breath.

Then she reaches right up high with her long long trunk and pushes away the clouds so the sun can come out and shine again.

They're leap leap leaping on the high sunny
hill because Lilliput is brave and bold,
and Strawberry Luca has found her shoe.

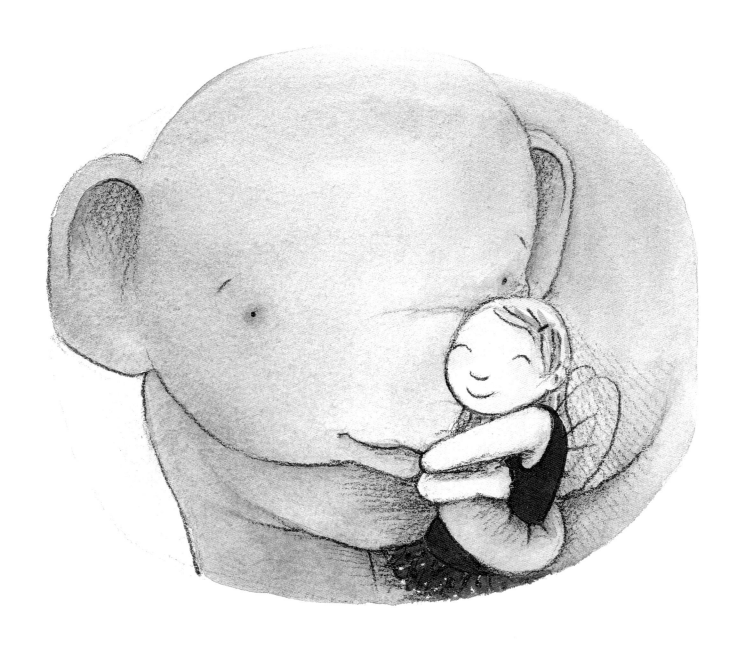

And Mannie likes to pull
noses of people she loves.

Now where are you going, Mannie?

'We're flip flop flying
down the long low slope.'

'We're tip top toeing along the dark pointy roofs . . .'

'Because it's time to go home.'

'And we're shoosh shhh shooshing
in our warm little bed.
Because now it's time for sleep.'